It's Okay to Ask!

Illustrated by
Nancy Carlson

Gillette Children's Specialty Healthcare • Saint Paul, Minnesota

This book is gratefully dedicated to the families of Gillette Children's Specialty Healthcare, who shared their experiences and made certain, first and foremost, that we wrote an honest book; to the writers, who provided language as simple and universal as that of a child; to the team at Gillette, who helped ensure technical accuracy; and to all of those who championed and helped shape this book.

This book is also dedicated to any child who's ever felt different—and to any parent who's ever been asked a question that is difficult to answer.

Gillette Children's Specialty Healthcare
200 University Avenue East
Saint Paul, MN 55101

www.gillettechildrens.org
www.curepity.org
Publications@gillettechildrens.com

Printed and bound in the United States of America

First Edition

LCCN 2014956633

ISBN 978-0-9862342-0-0 (hc.)

10 9 8 7 6 5 4 3 2 1

ISBN 978-0-9862342-1-7 (pbk.)

10 9 8 7 6 5 4 3 2 1

This book was expertly produced by Book Bridge Press.
www.bookbridgepress.com

You have lots of questions,
and that's okay.
You don't have to be scared,
or worried, or sad for us.
We are kids just like you.
So go ahead and ask!

Can your chair go fast?

Yes, my wheelchair goes pretty fast. It even helps me do ballet.

I am Maya, and I am

GRACEFUL!

Can we
play games on
your tablet?

My tablet has some games, but mostly it helps me talk and laugh and tell jokes.

I am Ahmed,
and I am
FUN!

Why was
6 afraid
of 7?
Because
7 8 9!

Why are those
on your legs?

These braces help me walk.
I can even run fast with them.

I am Tran,
and I am
ADVENTUROUS!

What is that?

This is a walker. I use it to get around, like to my favorite place, the library.

I am Gabriela,
and I am
SMART!

What kind of bike
is that?

This is a special bike
that helps me balance.
Let's go for a ride!

I am Carter,
and I am
FRIENDLY!

Now we have some questions for you!

Do you like nuts?

Would you rather read books or play outside?

What's your favorite dinosaur?

Here's the best question of all...

Do you want to be friends?

Read Aloud Discussion Guide

It's Okay to Ask! introduces kids to five friends who have disabilities or complex medical conditions. These young characters love to read, play, tell jokes, and make new friends. Use this guide to help your child see beyond a person's disability, develop an accepting attitude, and form positive opinions through friendship. As children ask questions and get to know the characters in this book, they will discover they are more alike than different, and that people of all abilities can be friends.

Before Reading

Read the title of the book and look at the cover: What do you see on the cover? Who are the people pictured? What are they doing? What do you think this book might be about?

Talk about friendship: What does it mean to be a friend? (Friends share interests, play, learn new things, and have fun together. They help each other, too.) What do you like to do with your friends?

Introduce the story: Have you ever been curious about people and asked them questions? In this book you will meet five new friends and some kids who are curious about them. Any time you have a question, remember it's okay to ask. Ready? Let's meet our new friends!

While Reading

Make predictions: When you meet each friend, a child asks a question. Before turning the page, ask: What do you think will happen next? What will the friends do? Where will they go? Will they be friends? Turn the page and read to find out. What happened? Did you guess? If not, what surprised you?

Notice similarities and differences: How are you the same as the kids in the book? Do you also like to dance, ride bikes, read? What else? How are you different? Do you spin on your toes while Maya spins on her wheels? Do you ride a two-wheel bike while Carter rides a three-wheel bike?

Reading Tips

- Relax and take your time reading.
- Let your child hold the book and turn the pages.
- Ask your child to describe what's on each page.
- Introduce vocabulary that names the devices the children use. (See Glossary of Terms.)
- Relate your discussion to your child's personal experiences.

After Reading

Ask questions about something different: Sometimes people can tell something is different about us, and sometimes they can't. We can see Gabriela needs her walker to help her get around, but we might be surprised to find out that Ahmed needs his tablet to talk because we couldn't see that at first. Kids are often curious about other people, and they might want to ask questions. Maybe you wear glasses or a hearing aid. Maybe you have a bandage, a cast, or stitches. When people first see you, what might they notice that is different about you? What can't they see that's different about you? What do they ask or say? How do you feel when they ask questions? Why? What would you like them to ask you?

Think about how health care providers help us: Doctors, nurses, physical therapists, and other health care providers help make our bodies stronger and healthier. Tran's doctors, nurses, and orthotists help him support his legs so he can walk and run better. Carter's physical therapist helps him get stronger so he can ride his adaptive bike. How has your doctor, nurse, or other health care provider helped you?

Discover what tools help us: Kids use all kinds of tools to help them do things. Maya uses a wheelchair to dance, and Ahmed uses a tablet to talk. What kinds of tools help you? Do you wear a helmet to protect your head when you ride your bike or scooter? Does your car seat protect you and help you see out the window? Do you have a backpack to help you carry your school supplies? Do you wear glasses to help you see better? Have you ever stood on a stool to help you reach high places?

Learn about making friends: Pretend that some of the kids in the book moved into your neighborhood and you want to be friends. What would you want to do with them? How would you invite them to play? What would you say?

Activities for Repeat Readings

- Read the book like a play. Ask your child to read one role (asking or answering) and you read the other.
- Play "I spy" in the park scene. Find and name the five friends. Find the butterfly, the dog, and so on.
- Describe the emotions expressed by each child and how those feelings later change.

About Gillette Children's Specialty Healthcare

Gillette Children's Specialty Healthcare is different from other children's hospitals for one simple reason: its focus. Gillette is a nationally and internationally recognized leader in the diagnosis and treatment of children, teens, and adults who have disabilities and complex medical conditions. It focuses on providing its patients with an exceptional depth of expertise rather than providing care for all pediatric conditions. Gillette patients have extensive needs and, in many cases, require lifelong care.

Gillette's main hospital campus is in Saint Paul, Minnesota, but its presence is felt everywhere. Gillette receives referrals from all fifty states and around the globe.

About CurePity®

The way people think about disabilities either creates opportunities or obstacles. Not long ago, many people believed that children who have disabilities couldn't attend school, play sports, or become active members of their communities.

Gillette has fought to establish and protect the rights of people who have disabilities by developing new medical treatments and technologies and by championing the CurePity movement.

The CurePity movement is a commitment to moving attitudes forward—away from pity and toward acceptance of kids who have disabilities or complex medical conditions. It's a pledge to support them with hope, courage, and expert medical care in a world that gives them a chance. Together we can move attitudes forward.

We must never lose sight of the past or cease imagining an even brighter future. By joining the CurePity movement, you join a legion of people committed to rejecting pity and taking action to move everyone forward. **Visit www.curepity.org to learn more.**

About CenturyLink

CenturyLink's vision is to improve lives, strengthen businesses, and connect communities by delivering advanced technologies and solutions with honest and personal service. CenturyLink extends this vision through volunteerism, contributions, and other collaboration with community organizations focused on K-12 education and programs that support youth, technology focused initiatives, and strengthening communities. In Minnesota, CenturyLink supports Gillette and CurePity advocacy through sponsorship of this book.

When CenturyLink learned about Gillette Children's Specialty Healthcare's CurePity movement in 2012, it knew it had found a cause that aligned with the organization's mission.

Since 2012, the company and its employees have supported CurePity through donations and volunteerism. In 2014, CenturyLink partnered with Gillette to launch CurePity Heroes, which recognizes people who have gone above and beyond to help create a better, more inclusive world for people who have disabilities or complex medical conditions.

About the Illustrator

Nancy Carlson has written and illustrated more than 60 picture books. Her specialty is teaching kids to feel good about themselves and others. Readers say they recognize themselves and their friends in the characters who triumph over everyday situations. Each story helps young readers deal with life while teaching the basic values of honesty, determination, and self-confidence.

Nancy lives in Minneapolis, Minnesota. She has three grown children and two granddaughters. Besides writing and illustrating children's books, she exhibits her artwork in various galleries and museums. You can check out Nancy's books and artwork on her website, www.nancycarlson.com, and follow her on Twitter and Facebook.

Glossary of Terms

Adaptive bike

A bike especially suited to fit a child's body and abilities. Children have many different abilities, so there are many different kinds of adaptive bikes. They help children have fun while they ride safely.

Leg braces (also called ankle-foot orthoses, or AFOs)

Custom-molded plastic braces that children wear around their lower legs to help them stand, walk, and run. Orthoses keep their ankle and foot in the correct position for better support. Some kids wear leg braces until their bones finish growing; others wear them longer. Children can choose fun decorations to put on their braces.

Motorized wheelchair (also called a power chair or electric wheelchair)

A mobile chair with wheels and brakes powered by a battery. It's made to fit each child's size. It's also made for left- or right-handed children so they can drive it themselves. Sometimes kids can carry their books and toys with them on the chair. Never push someone who uses a wheelchair without asking.

Tablet (also called an augmentative and alternative communication device, or ACC)

A small, easily carried computer that helps children talk and communicate. It uses letters, words, and symbols. The electronic voice says whatever the child enters on the tablet's screen.

Walker

A tool children use to help them balance or get support to make walking safer. They can put stickers or other decorations on it.